The Berenstain Bears®
and the
SUMMER JOB

Stan & Jan Berenstain

Reader's Digest **Kids**

Westport, Connecticut

It was summertime. School was closed for the year. Brother and Sister Bear were walking down a dusty road. They were thinking about how they should spend their summer vacation.

"We could just play," said Sister.

"Playing is fine," said Brother. "But playing all the time would be boring."

"We could go swimming," said Sister.

"Swimming is fine," said
Brother. "But we can't go
swimming every day."

"We could go to the library," said Sister.

"Yes," said Brother. "Mama takes us to the library every Saturday. But what will we do the rest of the week?"

"Maybe we could get a
job!" said Sister.

"That's a good idea," said
Brother. "But what kind of
job could we get? We're just
cubs."

That's when they saw the sign.
It was hanging on Farmer Ben's
front gate. It said: HELP WANTED.
SEE FARMER BEN.

"Well, yes," said Farmer Ben. "I do need help. But I was thinking of someone older. What could you cubs do to help?"

"All kinds of things,"
said the cubs.

"We could sweep the barn,

feed the chickens,

collect
the eggs,

"Hmmm," said Farmer Ben. He thought for a while. Then he said, "All right. The job is yours. Here are some brooms. You can start by sweeping the barn."

"There's just one thing," said Sister. "If this is a job, we should get paid."

"Yes," said Brother. "How much will you pay us?"

"Hmmm," said Ben. "See
that field? That's my cornfield,
and corn is my cash crop."

"What's a cash crop?" asked Sister. "A cash crop is what a farmer grows to make money," said Brother.

"I'll tell you what," said Ben. He took a piece of string and some sticks and marked off a corner of the field.

"If you do a good job, I'll pay you the money I get for all the corn that grows in that corner of the field."

"How much will that be?" asked Sister.

"Depends," said Farmer Ben.

"Depends on what?" asked Brother.

"Depends on getting rain," said Ben. "Not too little; not too much. Depends on cornbugs. In a bad year cornbugs can ruin a crop. Depends on keeping the crows from eating the seed—

that's why I'm making this scarecrow."

"So we won't know how much money we'll earn until the end of the summer," said Sister.

"No more than I will," said Farmer Ben. "That's the way it is with farming."

So the cubs

went to work.

They swept the barn.

They fed

the chickens.

They collected the eggs.

They slopped the hogs.

They called the cows. HERE BOSSIE

They made sure the bull pen was locked tight.

And they kept a close watch on their corner of the cornfield!

Brother watched the sky for rain.

Sister had bad dreams about cornbugs.

And when the crows
were no longer afraid of
Farmer Ben's scarecrow,
Brother and Sister made a
scarier one. It even scared
Farmer Ben.

Working on the farm was hard, but it was fun, too.

Brother and Sister made friends with the animals—

the chickens,

the pigs,

the cows.

Even Ben's big bull seemed
to like Brother and Sister.

But the best thing was having their own corner of the cornfield. The corn grew straight and tall and was filled with fine, fat ears of corn.

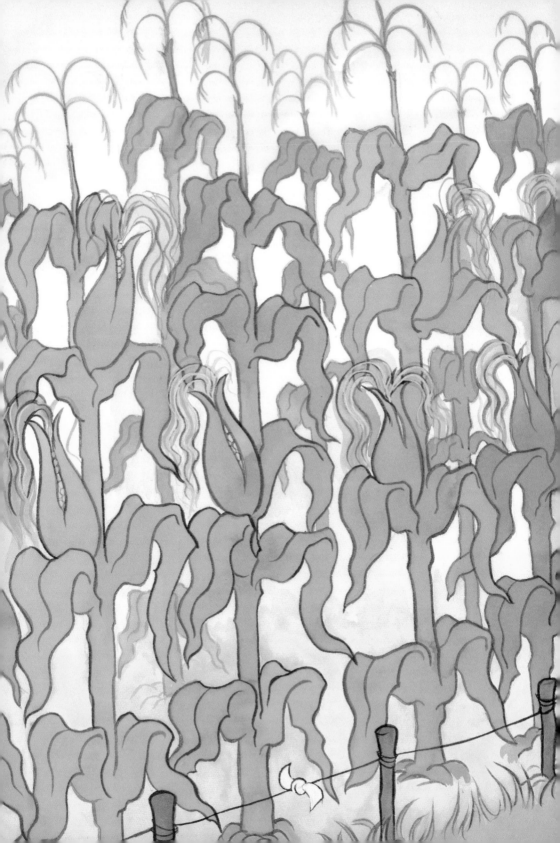

"Yessir," said Ben as he got ready to harvest the corn. "This is the finest cash crop I've grown in years. You cubs are going to do all right."

And they did. Their corner
of the cornfield earned them
many, many dollars.

"Well," said Farmer Ben. "Don't spend it all in one place."

"We won't," said Brother. "But we will *put* it all in one place—the bank!"

"That's right," said Sister. "It took us a long time to earn this money. We want to keep it at least as long as it took to earn it."